I0817636

Fiction / $20.00

“A nonlinear narrative which leaves one gasping at the power of the short burst woven into the larger tapestry. The cohesion of these dozens of disparate characters is testament to Chris Erickson’s ability to distill the essence of human quirk into one narrative that makes the heart ache and sing, all at the same time. *Henrytown* ushers in an exciting new voice in experimental literature.”

—Jacinda Townsend, author of *Trigger Warning*

“I’ve long wondered whether writers were out there who might take up the mantle of Derek McCormack’s spare, acidic humor, and relentless movement throughout equivalent bizarre tableaux. I’ve found McCormack’s logical heir in Chris Erickson’s brilliant, relentless *Henrytown*, a work as shifting and fragmented as the times, and as compelling a new voice as I’ve encountered in years.”

—Grant Maierhofer, author of *Traumnovelle*

“I don’t write blurbs, on gp. If I wrote blurbs, though, I would sure as fuck write one for *Henrytown*. I even considered violating my policy to do it, but imagine how many previous requesters this would piss off!”

—Joe Wenderoth, author of *Letters to Wendy’s*

HENRYTOWN

a novella by

Chris Erickson

Published by Dzanc Books,
in collaboration with Graver Goods Press

Dzanc Books
2580 Craig Rd.
Ann Arbor, MI 48103
www.dzancbooks.org

ISBN: 9781938603334
First edition: August 2025
Interior design by Michelle Dotter
Cover design by Chris Erickson

Printed in the United States of America

10 9 8 7 6 5 4 3 2 1

For Fred and for Henry

YETUNDE WAS STANDING holding baby Paco; he had on just his diaper. Yetunde said, "Where's your uncle Marty-Neil?" Paco looked, and you could see him looking. "Where's Uncle Marty-Neil at?" she said. Paco pointed at Marty-Neil Willard standing there; Marty-Neil gestured.

Yetunde said, "Where's baby Mustafa?" Paco moved his arm and finger and pointed at Mustafa being held by Henriette Lightbody with one arm; Henriette looked at Mustafa; Mustafa had on a blue, hooded suit.

Yetunde put her finger in Paco's hand; he squeezed it hard and made a triumph sound with his mouth.

ON ONE NIGHT IT WAS BAD WILLIE SLEMMONS in aisle six of the Star Market looking at frozen meals.

"Like an old fool angel he looks," thought Hwang the night manager, looking at Bad Willie. Hwang was holding a mop in his hands.

Now, Bad Willie Slemmons was a crippled individual. Had he two little decrepit arms, no elbows or hands, and only one little finger growing straight out of his right wrist. His dukeless arm—that was his left—appeared to be a vast, uncut wiener on the droop.

Despite his disability problems he had with his arms, he was still pretty good with a knife, he claimed. He had an eighteen-inch customized Jim Bowie. A Danville cutler had put a leather strap and fingerhole in the handle for him. When Bad Willie took and belted the weapon to his arm, he had to make sure to pull the strap through using his molar teeth on the right side of his head-mouth; his other teeth he had (few) were liable to come out; the looseness was caused by this rascal's chemical habits.

In any case, Bad Willie would have liked to doll that knife up in a man's gore for real, but, of course, civilization says you can't do that. Bad Willie Slemmons understood that. So, he worked around civilization's rules in two ways:

1) He a little bit threatened neighbors with the knife.
2) He introduced the knife into the sex act.

Let it be said that Bad Willie Slemmons did not substitute knife-for-his-regular wiener or cut down a sex collaborator during a coitus; all he did was point the knife at his collaborator and yell at his collaborator while he got pumped. Not to say yelling can't be hurtful to a collaborator, but my deal is, if you have to use a blade in your sex act, you should get permission from your collaborator before you do so, or at the very least, *warn* your collaborator. But, as you know, I am not Bad Willie Slemmons and neither are you.

Hwang looked, as he floated toward Bad Willie, at the young man's severely deformed person, which I have already described to you.

"It's—right now—it's between a meatloaf and chicken breast right now," Bad Willie said; spit flew off his mouth onto the glass door of the freezer. "Which ones *you* be eating?"

Hwang thought Bad Willie had the most high, beautiful voice. Hwang looked at the freezer and said he likes Healthy Choice. "The entrées are wonderful."

Bad Willie leered at Hwang. "You be working out?"

Hwang was looking at Bad Willie's arms. Hwang invited Bad Willie to take his time in selecting his meal: "There are many flavors," he suggested. Hey, that was Hwang—customer care was first to him. He goes, "I am just going to finish mopping this," but ultimately he stayed put, looking at Bad Willie's wrists. You could say he *remained.*

Bad Willie squared up to his man. He looked upon Hwang's business district for longer than one might expect. He was looking *right there.* He pushed back his glasses with his arm. His brain was communicating with his body capsule. His autonomic nervous system performed its office: *corpus cavernosum, look out*!

A thoroughgoing report on what you would have seen in Bad Willie's front left trouser pocket at that moment would have had to include the word *movement.* Bad Willie's mouth filled with spit; his head moved; his arms went forward.

Hwang wondered on the side: "In the grand scheme

of things, what does it mean to want to hold this man down and study his arms? To want to try gripping his wrists tightly and gently to see what the difference is? I will make notes about him in my private journal! Maybe I could take a shot at a poem-card…"

Bad Willie went with a Healthy Choice brand complete meal, like Hwang said to. But since the registers had been counted, Bad Willie couldn't pay—not even with his personal debit card. Hwang told him, "It's OK with me to take the item to sample. You can come again tomorrow and pay. Maybe at this same time. It's OK with me. I will be here regardless. I am closing tomorrow regardless." Bad Willie was standing there just taking it all in.

Next evening same time, Bad Willie showed up and got a bunch more Healthy Choice brand and paid via personal debit card. Hwang had already let Liza the checker go early; she was always asking to go early.

After a little standing around, Hwang and Bad Willie went for a bunch of coitus in the back office. All during, Bad Willie kept making this soft little warbling noise. Meantime, Healthy Choice brand in the bag, thawing out.

Hwang did have trouble gripping the floor with

his loafers on. It was kind of dusty in the office there. Hwang had to go barefoot so he could, you know what I mean, grip a little better on his different pumps, leverage his man better. And one point I do want to say is that when Hwang bent down to set his loafers and socks aside, Bad Willie's little bare moneymaker was there. *Right, right there.*

Cramped but organized accommodations. Everybody did OK. Stand-up deeds mostly.

Hwang did get to do his gripping experiment on Bad Willie's wrists and finger. It was great but, remarkably, he never wrote about it in his journal.

JOHN DINGER ON A DAVENPORT, knees sticking clear out in the room.

His uncle Milgotz was in the chair; Aunt Era was in the other chair. They had those two chairs, like that. They were fine to have John over even if they didn't know him that well.

Johnny Carson was on; Michael Landon was on there. They looked great. Landon said something to Johnny and looked at the audience; Johnny looked at the surface of his desk, then at the audience.

Era's little dog Ryan was standing by the davenport, vibrating; he had on his red nylon harness he wore all the time.

When John Dinger moved, Ryan looked and moved. When Dinger got up and went to the toilet when it was commercials, Ryan started vibrating uncontrollably.

PACO'S BIOLOGICAL WAS OVER his woman's taking his wiener indoors of her; the collaborators' skins stuck together and peeled apart on the different pumps.

Subsequent to withdrawal, Paco's Biological walked down Lula Mae Street with a can of beer. He was bare-chested and when he passed under the streetlamp, you could see his stomach for the soft, slickery brown area it was.

He went up till he come to Lamoille Park. He stood by the monkey bars awhile. He put his hand on a bar and, feeling it wet, slid his hand along there. He put his beer on the ground and tried to raise his thigh up to dry the bar on his cutoffs, but it was too tall to him. So, he undid his cutoffs, took them down, and stepped out of them. He wiped the monkey bar down with his cutoffs. His wiener kind of joggled around in the darkness a little bit while he did it.

He wiped his mouth, stomach, and undercarriage with the cutoffs before putting them back. He got up his can of beer and walked toward Bearing's horse stable on the west of town.

He felt his way from the road through the weeds to Jim Bearing's wire fence and leaned his arms on it. He saw two little horses standing together. He didn't know if they were mares or geldings or what; he didn't know because he couldn't see. He looked beyond the pasture area, across the bean field toward Polk Plastics. He could see the little lights way, way out there. The big male horse was standing by the fence not ten feet from him.

LADY BUTTON CHIPPED ICE OFF her driveway with a snow shovel. She had a half dozen clear dildos strapped on. And a few red ones, too; Christmas was coming.

GLORIA-HALF-OF-SOMETHING the wampus cat murdered Mandu Fam Lam Bartlum on a day in 2002. She ran him down behind the Park Tavern at Mineral, tore his head open to one side, pulled out his eyeballs, and cored out his rectum. She walked it over and placed his rectum in the parking lot. You couldn't tell what it was; it wasn't in the right context; and it was all kind of stretched out.

It was Queen Mother Brard with her male helper in front of the post office; they were standing holding their mail and communicating with each other. You could see them. Mandu Fam Lam went by on his nice dirt bike. He looked, and now Brard and them were looking up the street the other way.

Mandu Fam Lam Bartlum came to Uncle Forrey's visitation. He was standing near the casket looking at Forrey. Mandu Fam Lam had on a gorgeous blue sweater; there was fine embroidery all on it. He looked very beautiful to the family; they could never be through looking at him.

BIG JOHN DINGER CAME OUT of Esker's Tavern. He had gore on his fingers and sleeves. It was a big welt on his forehead. His hair was blowing around.

He was looking at the gore; it was freezing on his clothes. He tasted throw-up saliva coming on the side of his tongue. He crossed the highway and stood on Jim Bearing's property.

His fingers hurt from tearing down the urinal and pounding the person with it. He leaned over and threw up on the property. He kept shivering and throwing up in the snow two more times. His hair was moving.

He came across out of the ditch and saw it was glare ice on the asphalt. He got down and placed his fingers on the ice; he put all the different parts of his sore fingers. He was putting his hands. His hair was plastered to his head.

ALL RIGHT, Joshua Waughop the hunchback dwarf had a real limited set of magical powers he could do. I mean *real* limited. Some dwarfs can do metallurgy and everything else, but not Joshua. In fact, the only trick he *could* do in this world was conjure a little blue wagon and ride around in it.

And anyway, one day in '83, Joshua was eating a sack lunch in his little fort made out of blankets in the woods north of Edda Pond and thinking about what Rambo had done and said in the movie. Rambo had yelled in the movie, and Joshua thought about that, about Rambo yelling and *losing it*. Rambo was a guy who meant business; you could tell by how the authorities on there was reacting to Rambo. There was, of course, the part where he kept riding a dirt bike.

A little later, Joshua conjured his blue wagon and rode around in the woods like he never saw the movie.

MARTY-NEIL WILLARD WAS RIDING in Yetunde's hatchback. Marty-Neil's beard was *all over the place.* Yetunde was driving; her hairdo was hitting against the roof if she turned a certain way. Paco was in the back in his child seat trying to figure out how to word a question he had in his mind.

OK, Marty-Neil's seatbelt strap was under his beard, right exactly between his boobs. I want you to know that Marty-Neil had these real soft, bald boobs. He was hairy up and down his arms and legs and on his chest and back; and he pretty much had second and third beards on his frontal genital area and on his anus area, respectively.

But, you know, he had these soft little bald boobs.

The structuring on his was different from regular human boobs; his were more tube-like. They reminded me of the water snake novelty toy you can get at the fair, because if you pushed or squeezed one, the nipple part, or sometimes the whole other boob, would bulge out toward you.

But you never wanted to squeeze his boobs real

hard or handle them in a rough manner—you always *carefully took control* of Marty-Neil Willard's boobs.

You know when you go to touch regular boobs your fingers point up or maybe to the side, depending on your angle? Well, with Marty-Neil, you held your hand like you were going to shake hands, and then you gently curled your fingers under and around his boob like that. Actually, before you touched his boobs at all, you had to get his beard out of the way. But you always, *always* carefully took control of his soft little bald boobs. And you smiled warmly at him.

"Here we are, Mr. Five Years Old," Marty-Neil said, turning around in his seat to talk to Paco. Yetunde turned her vehicle into the Danville mall parking lot. Her hairdo made a little noise against the roof in that moment.

Marty-Neil had the impulse to get out and walk into Bergner's, tie his beard back, and empty a bottle of real fancy moisturizer all on his boobs. He would need to get away to do it, for his family members would feel bad seeing that kind of a scenario. They would recoil from that. Plus, he didn't know if he could bring himself to do it in front of them; he didn't think he could stay in the same frame of mind. But he didn't want to get away from them. He didn't want to be alone in Bergner's. He wanted them near him. He wanted to buy them nice things they wanted to have. *He also wanted pure white moisturizer to be upon every, single square inch of his boobs.*

From: John <fishburnej@yahoo.com>
To: Ads <ads@henrytowncrier.com>
Date: Thu, 30 Nov 2004 10:15:03
Subject: Advert Placement Quotes Needed

Dear Publisher,

I am John Fishburne The asigned Team instructor of the position available at TRANSCORP ELECTRONICS GROUP OF COMPANY. I will like to place an Advert in your paper for five weeks and will like to know the advert quote for the six weeks. Be Advised that payment will be via credit card and AD text is written below.

URGENT PART-TIME JOB OFFER AVAILABLE AT TRANSCORP ELECTRONICS GROUP OF COMPANY !!! Certified Payroll Specialist (CPS) that will be acting as Company's Account Manager, writing payment out to the Company's client is urgently needed. Monthly Salary:- $1500.00 Interested Applicant should get back to us immediately with their resumes via Email Address at: transcorpfirm@yahoo.com.

I want you to get back to me with the advert quotes for the five weeks as soon as possible so that I can forward my credit card details for the AD payment.

Name: John Fishburne
Company Name: TRANSCORP ELECTRONICS GROUP OF COMPANY
COMPANY'S ADDRESS: 119 Wayne Street
City : Omaha | State : Nebraska | Zip Code : 68046
Phone : (609) 394-2302

PILAR KUSNETSOV WOKE UP two in the morning to toilet. Her urinary bladder was full to pain. This was when she was carrying number seventeen baby Maddox Kusnetsov. Pilar was forty-six.

To toilet, her kidneys were sloshing around in her body capsule: One was up in front by her stomach by the baby; the other was behind a breast. Her liver went floating up her back. Her intestines came apart and went down in her leg.

Maddox was in the uterus area, where he lived at that time. He was pumping his legs and messing with the cord.

From: <ads@henrytowncrier.com>
To: John <fishburnej@yahoo.com>
Date: Tue, 2 Dec 2004 07:58:41
Subject: RE: Advert Placement Quotes Needed

Hi John,

We do not publish classified ads from outside our area. But I'm sure you can find great people in Omaha to work in the payroll department at Transport Electronics Group of Company.

Don't worry; Omaha is a great town.

Yours,

Carlier Johnson
Editor and Publisher
(217) 364-3250

carlier@henrytowncrier.com

THESE ONE SCHOLAR-NUNS had a debate going in front of Star Market:

"Uh-oh, looks like the lamp is burning!"

"Oh for chrissake."

"I completed vast practices and I make—*now I really make*—the call for universal love!"

"Oh for chrissake."

"*Do* you hear me calling?"

"Have you come to a debate or to share your TV slogans? Do you have supporting reasons?"

"I honestly straight-up *live* reasons now. That's my debate. Having completed vast practices, you know, my body is reasons. *All* this is reasons," and she made a general environmental gesture.

"I'll give you 'vast practices!'" and she looked like she was about to whack somebody.

"In and of itself it's all I need to begin calling and singing for you."

"I don't accept this."

"I done *done* vast practices regardless. They *been* handed down, handed down, all, to tell me one thing:

I'm no huckster on a town corner like you're treating me, and I'm not lying on you, and we *got* to have universal love up in here!" And, with that, this nun clapped her hands in front of the other's nose!

"Oh for chrissakes."

"How you like me *now*?"

"Careful now! And even you said 'now' before. Careful with 'now'! Don't act like you've *gained* or *become* now you're back from retreat! Don't act like anything happened. Vast practices don't need being 'handed down,' as you say. This would strictly be in the larger sense. Do you follow me?"

"I feel you."

"It follows that, as you say, your 'body' was 'reasons,' *before retreat*. So how did this get handed down?"

"Regardless if vast practices *been* being here, it *was* handed down, overstand. And it *was* transmitted because before I didn't start calling for it like I am! Like pure direct education."

"You must understand I'm not talking about someone explaining it to you, like, 'You should do vast practices and here's how you do it, because you will want to call for it all over and teach them…' That would just be somewhat conventional. You must understand I'm talking about *in the larger sense*."

"I feel you."

This nun looked dead serious: "It follows that you went on retreat, did vast practices, and nothing happened."

"You act like I'm entranced from retreat, and like I don't mean it. You act like I'm a corner huckster, like I'm lying on you. You act like there's no such thing as two things. You act like there's no effort. And this is like giving cutdowns to me!"

"I love you in a personal sense, welcome back to town, and hats off to you; I just don't ever in a million years think anything happened on retreat."

"Look at you you're all smug! You bring up 'the larger sense,' but your reaction is straight-up smallest scale. That's on the real *for real*."

"Can you prove you're not entranced from retreat?" Nuns around these two were having their own debates in the parking lot. It was a nice morning. The nuns felt fresh and alive. "You said 'you act' but *you* act out here, and flap your lips after your non-retreat full of nothing special!"

"My proof is the next ten thousand years of my behavior."

"Well, as long as you are thinking about the future, I think you're caught now and finished!" and she shut down her personal space.

YOU SAID NOBODY EVER MADE a dildo cape. You said.

Well, I guess it was vanity made you do that because there really was somebody... *who made a dildo cape.*

That's right, a dildo cape, d-i-l-d-o c-a-p-e, a cape of dildos.

Verily, starting in her twilight years, Lady Button had this thing where she liked to get strapped into a dildo harness. She enjoyed feeling the Naugahyde strap part under her buttocks area; she liked the weight of that PVC tackle hanging off the front. She was an anxious person, and it gave her comfort to do this, to get in a harness. Except, what happened I think, her mind got obsessed because it got to be where she would get into a harness first thing in the morning—even before cereal. She would go to the post office, harness on, with a dildo bent down somewhere under her coat; it would actually be *bent* down under there.

Then she kept ordering more and more dildos

every week: clear ones, red ones, flesh-colored ones, chocolate ones, glitter plastic ones, by and large they were in a Kong size. And she ordered harnesses for every one. And she put it on. I'm talking about she *put them all on*. She used to walk around inside her home with the dildos kind of sticking out.

As you're like to know (because you're a person), they make harnesses for about anywhere you want to have a dildo on yourself—you can put them all up and down. You know what, too, is they've been around since the Stone Age, dildos. They weren't as bendable back then because, you know.................but there you have it: Humans have been physically enjoying dildos for thousands of years.

Anyway, perhaps you can see Lady Button's line of thinking on this emerge, which was, "The sheer amount of dildos I have strapped to my head and body is directly proportional to the level of comfort I feel *with my emotions*."

Now to get to the dildo cape part. So, like any old normal day, Lady Button woke up and strapped on every harness and dildo she had. She walked into the hall. Right in front of the downstairs, her shoulder dildos knocked down several photographs from the wall, and she tried to look at that, but she got tangled up and went down hard. The dildos were heavy, but more than the gravitational force acting upon those dildos it was the fact that because it was harnesses all on her limbs she couldn't bend her joints. She couldn't *move*. Tough situation. But it worked out because it was at that time that she had the idea for the dildo cape. All right?

She pictured a huge, glaucous-blue vinyl cape with either mango tango or dollar bill trim. To actually get the dildos on the cape, she figured she would fasten little brass rings on there, make them even, space them out nice and even, drill brass hooks into the base of the dildos themselves, and then hook the dildos on the rings. This was the vision of it.

She said, "Yeah, you get your harnesses and your dildos going, then you stick a cape with a hundred dildos hanging off it over everything: *KA-BANG!! Twice as many dildos right there!*" She was talking out loud to herself, pretty much shouting like I was just doing. But, of course, her speech was a little bit muffled because there were a great many dildos across her mouth.

D-i-l-d-o. C-a-p-e.

Well, you know, my hope is now you don't feel so good. I don't know exactly *why* I hope that; I just want that for you.

HENRIETTE LIGHTBODY WAS OVER YETUNDE'S having coffee.

"He isn't one of these ones that like big women," Henriette said.

"He's little," Yetunde said. "It's little ones that do."

"How *you* know? You're little."

"I know, and I like big men."

"That's what *I'm* saying," Henriette said. "Because I never saw you with a little one yourself."

"I'm saying I know *him*, and he does," Yetunde said, having coffee. She looked at the placemat; she looked at Henriette.

Henriette had some coffee. She looked at the sweet rolls; she was breathing from her mouth and steady looking at the sweet rolls. Her bottom teeth were sticking out. "I'm *saying*," she said.

MAYOR SPEEDY KUSNETSOV'S TOOTHBRUSH had mashed bristles.

He would stand at the sink with his knees oh-so-slightly bent and rake the brush across his teeth hard as he possibly could, stripping off enamel rods like siding. The brush often slipped out of his mouth and suds got on his chin and sometimes even on his throat area.

It was textbook how *not to do* something.

Because of these efforts over many years, his gums got shoved up and back and you could see more of his teeth than you're really supposed to. Not a great situation in terms of, you know, the oral stuff.

When the dentist told Speedy maybe stop brushing his teeth so hard, Speedy raised off the arm rests and goes, "I'm mayor! Lot of people depends on me. I got lot of duties. People breathe down my neck twenty-four seven about every problem: 'Mayor, please do not levy tax! Mayor, get please livestock fences! Fix pothole,' on and on, day to night. Eh? I look to interests of citizen. That's is what is being public servant all about!

"But *you*, you don't know jack about it. What do *you* do? Pry mouth open? Yell at guy because gum push back? *I am mayor*! You breathe down my neck because gum? Big deal, asshole! Get life! Get real!"

Speedy's head was shaking violently, and he was leaning forward bearing his teeth like a wild animal at the dentist.

He continued: "Is not enough to you I run town so you can have bed, have little business, pry mouth, and no brick come in window? Tire slash? Bandits attacking? Without tank in streets and rabble rouse? And evidently somehow that's is not enough for you? I give and give and give and *give*, and you take, take, take, *take*—me, me, me, *me*! Eh? This is not Soviet Union! You cannot insult mayor!"

Speedy was holding his arms up in the air. His face and body capsule were real red and extra hot. He looked at the carpet while he lowered his arms.

The dentist was used to this kind of an outburst. His patients hated him. They believed he was an agent of evil. He wasn't; neither was his hygienist; neither was his administrative assistant.

Table 1. PVC Manufacturing accidents involving inadvertent reactor discharge

Year	Place	Cause	Result
1961	Japan	Contents of wrong reactor discharged.	Four killed, eight injured in plant and two outside. Major structural damage to the plant.
1966	New Jersey	Operator opened wrong reactor bottom valve, discharging contents.	One killed. Plant destroyed.
1980	Massachusetts	Operator opened wrong bottom valve, discharging fresh batch.	Two injured; damage over $1 million.
1980	California	Improper valve design allowed a bottom valve to remain partially open.	Major damage to the plant.

OUT IN THE VILLAGE OF NIANTIC, on the side of their gob pile, you could see a huge figure the size of a dinosaur running up and down. Long ago, they paid the famous troll-killer Big Bob a hundred dollars to go get rid of the figure. You know how it can be. So, Big Bob put on his famous burlap battle helmet and went up. But he come back down after an hour saying he hadn't seen anything up there. A smart-aleck villager came up to Big Bob, pointed at the figure in the distance still pacing upon the gob pile, and asked him if he needed glasses. Whereupon, Big Bob *destroyed* the villager and rode back to Henrytown.

They say Big Bob was the best troll-killer you ever saw; he had this nelson he'd do. He was a great big sexy kind of guy. He wore his hair in a beautiful low fade, and he had great skin.

He always had suggestions for you, or a request. Like if you went up to his place, before he'd invite you in, he'd ask you how you got there, what route you took from town. He'd look out and tell you another way to get there for next time. Sometimes he'd make observations about your clothing, this kind of thing. On your way out, he'd give you a clock-radio, or some gadget, maybe a boombox, and ask you to take it in for repair since you were going right by there. He'd be standing there, holding the boombox, and looking into your eyes. What could you do? He was *awesome.*

Big Bob loved holding things in his hands, like rabbits or a damn boombox. He liked to yell at people right in the ear. He liked biscuits and would sometimes toss them at people as a goof. Now there's something that hasn't been documented too much: the way old Big Bob of the 116th would sometimes toss biscuits at people as a goof. He never learned your name; he called everybody "Brian." He even called God "Brian," but he wasn't a religious man. Once, a neighbor asked Big Bob if he believed in God, and he picked up a biscuit and tossed it at the neighbor.

They say he killed five thousand Confederate cattle using that nelson he'd do. He'd draw up and execute the nelson, and the animal would sit there and die. One thing about him, the Army never issued Big Bob a uniform. Never-you-mind he was too big for one; they just didn't want him to have one, to ever *be in one.* Nobody wanted to have to see him in one, for they loved him too much. They said he could just wear whatever. He had this kind of weird, tan jacket he wore all the time, plus his famous burlap helmet. He was just a really physical guy.

After the war, Big Bob came back and settled outside Henrytown and, using his nelson, killed every troll in a hundred miles (plus their cattle). He was a pretty good-natured guy; when he stormed a troll village, he always spared their infants and children. He took them and kept them out at his place and brought them up himself. He always had land in those days. He used to walk his bean fields with the troll-children, always telling them he was not their natural father.

"I'm not your real daddy," he would say. "Forget about what you heard against that. If they tell you different, tell me, and I will kill they ass."

JOHN DINGER CAME OUT of Star Market; dew point: 39°F.

"Where *you* about to go?" Bad Willie Slemmons said; he was standing in the darkness.

Dinger looked at him. Bad Willie appeared to be eating. Dinger went toward him; he could hear eating.

"Where old-girl at?" Bad Willie said. All the sudden, as he said this, he dropped the food on the pavement. He knelt down to pick it up; his stump and finger touched the food that was on the pavement. The food had all come apart.

Yetunde came out of Star Market and went toward her Metro.

"There she go right there," Bad Willie said with some effort; food was stuck in the folds of skin on his stump. Dinger went toward the Metro.

UPON ONE PART OF THE LOCATION was John Dinger; Bad Willie Slemmons was upon another. Somebody with a flashlight walked by.

The old lawyer appeared in the sky about two hundred feet above Dinger's head. The lawyer was glowing bluish and so was his briefcase he had; legal documents to do with a deceased man were within the case; the legal documents themselves were *not* glowing.

The lawyer floated slowly upward; he looked pretty pleased with himself. He disappeared into stratus opacus uniformis clouds.

Six hundred million bushels of soybeans appeared over Bad Willie's head. Now, in terms of elevation, the beans were about where the lawyer had been, but, obviously, the beans took up more room than the lawyer ever did. Yeah, beans miles back of Bad Willie's head, clear to Bement, it looked like.

After a minute, the beans floated upward into the clouds.

Dinger and Bad Willie were, I don't know, seventy-five feet apart.

Dinger, suddenly wearing a different shirt, waved his arms around and issued verbal taunts to Bad Willie; the latter got his knife out and belted it to his stump. He held it in the air and looked.

Jens Kujawa appeared over Dinger; Jens Kujawa was glowing a little bit.

Dory Funk Sr, Dory Funk Jr, and Terry Funk appeared over Bad Willie. The Funks issued verbal taunts to Jens Kujawa and made gestures. The Funks were all trying to breaststroke in the air over to Jens Kujawa; presumably, they wanted to get over there and throttle him.

Meanwhile, Jens Kujawa looked like he didn't know where he was at; he was turned the other way; he had to kind of flail so he could see wherefrom the verbal taunts were being issued. Jens Kujawa looked down at Dinger. Kujawa and the Funks drifted up.

Highway to Heaven appeared over Dinger's head. Bad Willie looked at *Highway to Heaven*'s windblown hair. Bad Willie squealed and burst into tears. *Highway to Heaven* turned and looked down at him. Bad Willie wiped his eyes and nose on the folded-up wrist part of his jacket sleeve.

A brightly glowing toddler appeared twenty feet over Bad Willie's head. Dinger looked. The toddler looked discouraged; she was floating upwards.

In the other part of the sky, *Highway to Heaven* pointed at the toddler; the toddler pointed back at *Highway to Heaven*; *Highway to Heaven* laughed and asked the toddler if she wanted some juice. Dinger was staring at the toddler best he could.

Bad Willie wanted to walk up, climb up, and ram his knife blade in Dinger's throat area. He wanted Dinger's gore to all the time be showering his person and for it to coat the ground. He wanted his glasses and body to float in the gore; he wanted to dunk his chin in it and let it run in over his labium inferius oris and around his lateral incisor.

PILAR AND SPEEDY KUSNETSOV WAS PREGNANT a long time. And I can't think of one single, solitary reason not to list off all of their children for you.

They are as follows: Madison, Clayton, Hunter, Haley, Jordan, Tristan, Brenda, Ian, Chase, Megan, Mackenzie, Maddox, Asher, Cody, Gage, Brooke, Brodie, Tiffany, Braden, Courtney, Jennifer, Kaley, Amber, Skylar, Reagan, Jayden, Riley, Connor.

Good kids—all of them. I'm very sorry to say a small number of them are no longer with us. I'll check my notes for exactly which ones, and then I'll email you.

CARL THE MINI-DONK DIDN'T know the Fujita-Pearson Tornado Intensity Scale from a hole in the ground.

He went and stood by the well. The actual way he had his body oriented in relationship to the well made it look like he was looking at the side of the well. I don't know if he was or not. I don't know what he was doing. He was an old barn donk. He was not a circuit donk.

In the air above Carl were stratus opacus uniformis clouds. Pretty soon, that old W appeared in the corner of the TV, and some nimbostratus opacus clouds rode in. The family come and took Carl to the cellar. Pretty soon, a tornado formed and resulted and the well got ripped out of the ground.

Carl was still fine. As I specifically mentioned, he was in the cellar. In fact, he saw about a few turnips while he was down there. Joining Carl in the root cellar were the rest of the Bearing family: Jim, Graciela, Humph, Sis, Gizmo the pygmy goat, Janet the cat, and Private First Class Wilberforce Burlingame Laudermilke Jr. Jr. the basset hound. All fine.

One of Bearing's geldings got killed—his head had got in the way of an airborne chunk of the well after the barn had got ripped down.

When they were let out of the cellar, Carl and Gizmo went and stood by the hole where the well had been. Bearing was standing looking at his dead horse.

OK, my point in telling about Carl is, if you literally spread out a Fujita-Pearson Tornado Intensity Scale by that hole and then repositioned Carl the mini-donk so he could see both the hole and the Fujita-Pearson, he would not have known the difference.

HENRYTOWN CRIER

JULY 21, 1949:

The body of Ronald Bearing, a 17-year-old boy of Henrytown, was recovered by police from the Little Sugar River at New Glarus, Wisconsin this last Monday.

A bridge painting crew supervised by J.P. Bearing, Ronald's father, had been up there on a job, when Ronald, an apprentice on the crew, was accidentally struck in the head by a sandblasting hose, knocked into the river, and drowned.

The body will be returned to town this week for burial at Sherwood Cemetery. Pflum & Sons Funeral Home is in charge of arrangements.

PACO IN HIS NYLON JACKET standing in the backyard with a stick in his hand whipping leaves on the ground.

Yetunde come to the back door and told him time for school. He kept whipping the leaves a bunch of times until she told him again. She give him a dollar fifty hot lunch money.

Paco whipped the leaves on the walk to school. His totebag swung around and made him lose balance at times. His hand was all red. He put two hands on the stick and went into a chopping motion.

Many of the different Kusnetsov children were standing there holding lunchboxes and totebags, looking at this performance unfold, and feeding off the emotion of the situation.

Barometer: 29.992 in., falling; here come from Canada a trough, a front.

A leaf got stuck on the end of the stick; Paco was using the same stick as before, the one from his house. He said something to the Kusnetsov children. He removed the leaf with his hand, and then completely whipped the shit out of a pile of leaves.

MAIN CASE.

Bad Willie and Hwang enjoying biscuits and gravy over Hwang's in 1993, when suddenly and from nowhere, a huge robot bashes through the wall and walks into the kitchen and stands there vibrating, smoke pouring out of the eye sockets. The knees melt in and the robot falls forward and its massive head goes through the shabby chic table and everything just kind of smolders.

Bad Willie holds up his finger in the air.

COMMENTARY.

Poor design. The intense heat produced by the mechanical workings of that 'bot's intricate or semi-intricate innards was not allowed to escape, so she melted right in front of our boys' eyes. I would have gone for some gigantic vents in the side of it. Anyhow, we're left asking, "What was its mission?" What was its mission.

SPEEDY KUSNETSOV WAS SLEEP FACEDOWN in the creek back of Polk Plastics with snorkel gear strapped onto his head. Suds were all across on his head and on the snorkel itself. He was all set with his lifejacket and waterwings and his knees dragging in the bottom.

It was this three or four inches of exposed skin above his snorkel mask but below his hairline (his hairline started about at his coronal suture); mosquitoes kept biting into his head right there. Right there, *right there*.................in front of his hairline.

It—*that*, you see, *that*—was a system. That was a system.

Speedy's hair looked like the carpet right inside the front door; his hair was floating. *He was floating.*

His bathrobe was hanging on the transmission tower by the creek; and so was the bath towel from home.

His 1976 Lincoln Continental Mark IV Bill Blass Edition was parked in the field by there; the car was obviously extremely wide and long; obviously, he had some personal belongings in it, like documents and his billfold.

From: kluber Power Plant <kluberpowerplant@gmail.com>
To: Ads <ads@henrytowncrier.com>
Date: Thu, 19 Jun 2008 13:53:17
Subject: Sales/Clerk role Ad

Dear Sir/Madam

I will like to place a liner advertisement to go under the classified section of all your Newspaper publications and here is the ad to go:

Kluber Power Plant seek people to take the vacant position of Sales/Clerk role.For further info please send your resume to kluberpowerplant@yahoo.com

Please do get back to me with the total cost for the ad to run in all your newspaper publications per week

Best Regards
Donald Kluber

Kluber Power Plant
4134 W. California Ave
Phoenix,AZ 85016

206-611-4566

OUT FORT DANIEL CONSERVATION AREA, where they practiced their Nordic combined, a hag stood, going, up under *Quercus muehlenbergii*, going, “I know how a champion thinks; I am a world’s champion,” up under the ramp really going, “I can make you all champions.”

From: Ads <ads@henrytowncrier.com>
To: kluber Power Plant <kluberpowerplant@gmail.com>
Date: Fri, 20 Jun 2008 08:06:03
Subject: RE: Sales/Clerk role Ad

Hi Donald,

We are not accepting classified ad submissions from outside our area at this time. Be advised that your ad will not be published in our paper.

Please call me with any questions. Good luck with your power plant.

Yours,

Carlier Johnson
Editor and Publisher
(217) 364-3250

carlier@henrytowncrier.com

ONE ACTUAL LOCAL GEEZER NAMED MISTY in an elaborate opera cape with botanical motifs went for a walk across the entire community expanse felt safe. Misty did not feel disturbed. Misty walked along smoking not having difficulties and did not feel hounded and did not feel bitched-at. Misty did not feel violated by the community or attacked. Misty did not have devilment up in her face. Did not get knocked down in the street, or was not beaten. Was not smashed in the back of the head and lose her memory. Clothes did not get wet and muddy and frozen. The weather was great for Misty; weather did not turn. Businesses like the gas station were open and staffed in Henrytown. Misty saw community members at the gas station interacting in positive ways. It did not get too chilly. Misty saw Esker's. No one was really speeding through the streets. The people were kind to Misty. Not windy calm winds light and variable. The great geezer Misty did not have difficulty. There were no mix-ups. The geezer had a lovely walk. The geezer was charmed and delighted.

Misty the geezer walked across a huge expanse beyond town. Everything had no difficulties. Thinking strong, and not having difficulties whatsoever. A walk can be so much fun for a great little geezer like Misty like this! Acrosst a massive expanse beyond the gas station, beyond Esker's, no difficulties. The geezer Misty came to a crick and series of larger rock-like boulders. Geezer Misty looked at the boulders being in such a good feeling mood during the walk. She looks at the several rock-like rocks or slabs across a massive expanse nonstop almost looking like she's investigating it, or looking closely at, the rocks or boulders. She is hoping to find something to connect back to her recent. The recent walk was so positive for its effect upon Misty's mind. Looking to connect something back something to refer to to look back upon and to refer to, attempting to extend the feeling of the walk which was so positive no difficulties, no rip-offs, great weather, no mix-ups. She closely studied she sought to connect.

"What are even these big, shitty-butt rocks doing here? . . . . . Can't tell where I am no more," and the geezer looked around at the community expanse which had characteristics like a shitty little mountain and a shitty little fish pond in the opposite direction.

Misty, who was a geezer, pulled the opera cape around to see it: "Wish I never got this cape . . . . . . This cape can't help me in any way, and I regret getting it. I regret getting this bullshit-ass cape. I'd rather wear a hundred other things." Back to studying. A shitty-ass tree over there, OK. Misty started to take her weave out partway. Things turning.

Sundown the geezer walked between the boulders and megaliths. But then a part was hanging out and she slammed her kneecap and fell in silence. A very terrible injury had just occurred. Poor little Misty a geezer was so weak after it she didn't want to reach and touch her kneecap that much and she frankly didn't even see the point.

When she closed her eyes, she saw unstaffed businesses in her mind. She saw children doing things to put themselves in deadly danger, and she saw herself unable to help in that moment, and she saw herself conducting a fruitless visual scan of this community area for someone that could. She could find no young person to help. Instead, she saw young people elsewhere causing all devilment. Just all a bunch of things that the injury made her worry.

The expanse was silent. Misty thought local demonesses now seemed to be closing in on her consciousness. If she (Misty) had some energy she wanted to get her weave out if possible. She feared the demonesses of her mind were covering her mind and how would she retrieve it. She felt they wanted to control her mind and perhaps kidnap it to their prison cells for eons. She thought she better kind of make some noises to subdue them in her mind; she went for her weave and groaned loudly.

The opera cape had flapped up during the injury. The fabric had got flapped up and bunched on her shoulder. Misty saw part, and now she could see the botanical motifs' outlines. And now it was dark out, so all that was visible was the botanical motifs' outlines, the whole opera cape so elaborate, so over-the-top, *so Misty, so her*. The whole design no longer just part.

MOST TIMES, Pilar rode Speedy as kind of an organizational necessity after they hit fifty—well, forty-five. But now, Speedy wanted to get on there and get going. He couldn't help it. He was overcome.

His body capsule was a red-hot, slickery weight. His face-head was buried in the pillow over her shoulder; he turned or lifted to the side to get air. Stuff was coming out of his mouth; her hair was sticking into his mouth. His arms were under her. His feet were hooking on the end of the bed so he could get power, fitful power. Occasionally, he moved his buttocks in a circle to the one side.

For clear reasons, my mind turns to the subject of leverage. I saw an ad in the Danville paper just now that says the key to huge investment gains is leveraging your money—what the experts call *nondirectional trading*. That is, you don't necessarily look to buy stocks on the ground floor and hope they go up like you did in the old days; no, what you do now is "leverage" your money using a particular system or perhaps *systems*, depending. And it's in no actual direction. And timing doesn't matter; it is *beyond timing*. It's just pure leverage. Let that sink in. It's like he says in the ad: *"It's all about leverage!"* Had the italics and the exclamation point in there to show he means it, too.

Now, let me be perfectly clear to you about this: I know what "leveraging" is, but I don't care to learn more at the guy's free workshop at Prairie Capitol Convention Center, April 26-28.

LADY BUTTON WENT FOR FIREWOOD with some nice-sized clear dildos strapped on.

BIG GRIMY FREIGHT TRAIN like nobody's business, through town hard and slow forwards, on its way to Polk Plastics, where they turned out PVC resin to eventually make debit cards, traffic cones, dildos, carpet backing, and so on.

Waiting for it at Bess and Second, you had the village lawyer in his '90 LeBaron. The lawyer's neck muscles were hard because that was his powerhouse. When he wanted fire in a courtroom, he got it out of his neck, *to the back part of his neck*. That was a system in his life. The other parts of his body capsule tended to be nice and soft.

His belly neared the bottom portion of the steering wheel. He rubbed his tongue upon the gold crowns on the top molars located on the right side of his face-mouth, and it made him remember Cloris Barcewski, an old probate client. She was calling the office all the time at that time. One big concern was the money from her dead mother's gold crowns and fillings. She had had them pried out and auctioned off on the International Internet. She'd seen this commercial.

Getting the fillings sold appeared to be a heartless idea, but Cloris needed money. Like she told the lawyer, *she* was the one took care of Mother after the hip and all the way to the end after that. It wasn't her brothers; they didn't come around for it. They didn't want to know. "Put her in the home," he said. "You can put her in the home."

You see, one night her mother stepped out of the tub and went down like scrap metal. The hip went. The hip always goes, *has to go*. Subsequently, Cloris quit her job and moved in the house to care for Mother. And *she* kept track of the pills and drove Mother to the post office and the doctor's. *She* fed Mother. *She* physically got in the tub and washed out Mother's body with a washcloth; *she* washed the holes, washed the boobs in there, shampooed her hair. Cloris spoke to Mother as she stood upon the carpet and looked, looked. Coming out of dining area, looking, looking. Wearing jacket...wearing jacket.........wearing jacket....................................wearing jacket...... ....down to the end.

Now once Mother died, you should have seen Cloris' brothers come out of nowhere. They got real involved now. They wanted to know everything and, especially, get a look at The Will. By that time, they'd been cut out. They kept saying Cloris got Mother doped up on painkillers and had her cut them out down the stretch. One brother was able to cry on command like a movie star. He was the one Cloris said stole the cash from Mother's coffee can under the bed while she was in the nursing home with the hip. Tad was his name.

Well, on the appointed court day, the lawyer rode in LeBaron, went into his neck, and went after Tad. Tad was trying to get some tears going, but it wasn't like usual for some reason. He couldn't seem to execute with that lawyer getting after him. Pretty soon, Tad had the idea to act like he was going blind; he was sitting in the witness box reaching outward with his hands and whimpering, saying all he could see anymore was darkness. The judge was cold looking over. When that didn't shake out, the Tadder decided he'd lean forward and have some kind of convulsion. Case closed, pretty much.

The lawyer leaned his head and looked at the train driver; the driver had his arm hanging out the window; the lawyer looked at arm. Air went from the heating vents directly into the lawyer's nose and mouth, and his belly pressed against the bottom portion of the steering wheel and enfolded it.

D306
D308
D310
D312

OLD LOOKY COMING ALONG the asphalt on his adult tricycle, like he liked. I'm standing there.

Something lifted Looky into the air. There was a *lifting*. He was being *lifted* off the asphalt like he was rigged up to wires.

He was floating slowly over the earth; it looked like *he* believed this was normal. He kept floating and pedaling like he was on the asphalt. He was acting like he didn't think it was anything, but I can tell you: it was just like something was going on, like it was *an event of some kind*.

Pretty soon he was placed roughly back on the road. I saw this and heard the noise of this. He was on his side; the tricycle (his *weapon*) was on its side. I go over. There were hair clippings on his shirt. He got up passionately and picked up his weapon. There were leaves everywhere. He had a passion burning in his mind. Leaves were all over the place, in our hair. I'm standing there; it was even leaves *inside of my helmet*.

ANIGHT, Marty-Neil Willard, Paco, and John Dinger in Bombay Bicycle Club at Danville; they were *in the restaurant.*

Dinger got the $10.99 all-you-could-eat fried shrimp special. That won't surprise anybody. That wasn't a buffet special, by the way; it was a thing where you told the waitress when you wanted more, and she brought it out to you on a new plate, which, literally (in reality), made it more like an all-the-waitress-is-willing-to-bring-you shrimp system instead of a true all-you-could-eat.

Well, what happened after four hours of bringing shrimp to John Dinger, the waitress got to where she had had it, and she told the restaurant manager she wasn't going to bring out any more plates. She said she had to get home to her children. Her throat area was all red; she was about gonna have a meltdown.

The restaurant manager came over to the table. He was standing there; his pants didn't really fit him too well, if you looked.

Dinger was in the chair, knees higher than the

table. "I'm eating still," he said. "I didn't eat all I could eat yet."

"I know, but we *been* closed," the restaurant manager said. He kind of fidgeted with his pants. "And you can't have a forty in here," he pointed at Marty-Neil's bottle he had with him.

The restaurant manager looked at Dinger and Marty-Neil for about fifteen seconds; it was a kind of tactic. If the tactic didn't turn out, he had a plastic helmet in his office he could go put on. Or he could get his lawyer on the phone. He looked around and went over by the front door and looked out.

John Dinger got up from the table; his gigantic buttocks was asleep; his pants were drooping off there. He had his trunk over the table; he was waiting for the feeling to come back.

STREET RON DIED SITTING IN A CHAIR while listening to The Bhagwan; this was down in The Bhagwan's homeland.

The Bhagwan was pretty keyed up; he was touching his fingers together and looking around the wigwam at everybody. He was lecturing his followers on the mind, and he was *locked in.* You can go on however you want about him, but when it came time to lecture, The Bhagwan had his hardhat and lunch pail. By the way, he was seated in a massive, massive upholstered chair; if you looked from the side, you couldn't even hardly see him over the side of it. You couldn't see that that was even The Bhagwan. It was just, if you knew the chair you would know.

Everyone was listening carefully. Pretty soon, your man Street died and fell out of his chair. What happened basically, he died and slid down and outward, and the chair cold tilted forward up against Street.

They looked; The Bhagwan looked. Someone, a man—a man by the name of Wei Yu—also a follower of The Bhagwan, burst into song. He was leaned back; he had the most high, most beautiful voice and everything.

EVERYBODY out in Henrytown was black, if you ask me.

JOHN DINGER FROM POLK after work in the morning. Deer ran out in the highway. He moved his head and looked at the animals. It was astronomical dawn out. He was steady looking. More deer ran out. He plowed into the animals; one flew up the windshield and over.

He pulled over and got out and looked at what had happened. He went around; it was its hair sticking in the headlamp. He touched; he had his pan ten inches away from it. His head. He was bent down. He could see the one deer trying to get up off the pavement. He could hear it. The other animals were gone.

He heard something behind him, and he got knocked down hard and hit his head against the pavement and slid across.

Dinger looked over and beheld Gloria-half-of-something, the wampus cat. She was looking at him. She got into his LeSabre and ripped the upholstery. She was ripping the upholstery with her claws. She started slamming around, ripping upholstery, and slapping her paws on the dash. The horn went off several times; napkins fell out of the car.

Dinger crawled upon the pavement; he had a big cut on the side of his head; his hair was sticking out where blood was dripping. Gloria-half-of-something had her knees on the driver's seat, and she pushed her back up against the headliner and screamed. The radio cut on, and a hit song started playing so loud it was all kind of garbled. If you listened to it, it was that old "Whip Appeal." Napkins were blowing on the pavement, and it *was* that old "Whip Appeal."

Dinger looked at Gloria-half-of-something's bare buttocks sticking up; her top half of her body was a wildcat and her bottom half was a woman. He was looking to see. He was trying to get around to get the angle. It was a open wound on her leg he saw. She kept slamming her back on the ceiling, making the dome light go on and off. She would turn and look; and he was *steady* looking.

A ONE LOOK at Bad Willie's spoiled underpants and Hwang knew he had to get the borax to get the job done. Bad Willie had hidden the underpants in the hamper under some other clothing; he'd placed them so the bad part wouldn't touch the other clothing.

Hwang poured the borax in the wash; the box was completely upside-down when he did this. He wanted to overwhelm the underpants. He had that box like this; he was shaking it. He took his finger and tore the side spout open wider. Hot water was coming in on top of the underpants.

MARTY-NEIL WILLARD ON HIS PROPERTY eleven years before he died. Him and a Fred Bunnage—close quarters between the woodpile and the home.

"Incidentally, my name is Fred Bunnage," said Fred Bunnage, making that *tremendous* eye contact, "and I've been having these, sort of, very, *very* clear thoughts about you, Marty."

"How do *I* know what you're doing?" Marty-Neil said, looking at him.

To emphasize out-and-out *clearness*, Fred Bunnage spun his hands like propellers hard as he possibly could. Marty-Neil stepped back; Fred's hand clipped the siding. Fred's arm came apart and fell onto the cement. The fingers had come off. He looked. "My hand, Marty," he said, trembling. He bent down to pick it up; you could hear his shoes on the cement. "How will I think clearly about you *now*?"

Fred took his stocking hat off and put his hand and fingers in it; his hair was sticking out. He was crying and whispering into the hat. He stood up and gestured, reached out toward Marty-Neil. Eye contact: Off Of The Charts.

Later that evening, Fred bought a sub-zero sleeping bag on sale, came back, got in the bag, zipped up the bag, and wedged in under Marty-Neil's woodrack. He had the stocking hat with everything in it under his sweatshirt, against his stomach.

You had some overnight flurries; it wasn't much accumulation; maybe a butthair—*maybe* a butthair.

QUEEN MOTHER BRARD and her male helper drove into Danville to the Bonanza. She kept making a big deal about being there. She put their meals on her Senior Club Card.

Her helper went into the restroom and placed his headdress by the sink. He pointed his wiener down in the toilet. He went to the bathroom inside the toilet. He was holding his wiener in his fingers. He came over by the sink and brushed his hair.

When he came out he saw Queen Mother going toward the salad bar. He went and placed his headdress at their table. He looked and saw Queen Mother at the salad bar holding their plates. The lights over the salad bar were blinding. He fixed his silken cravat. He walked over there. She said something to him about what she wanted on her salad. There was a glare coming off the metal surface of the salad bar. He looked at the salad bar. He leaned toward the salad bar. His rear end was clamped together. He couldn't really see. He tried looking back toward their table but it was a wall right there; it was patrons right there. He hung onto the corner of the salad bar. The food looked like it was laser beams.

CARLIER'S HAIR SYSTEM came off and blew down the pavement; you could see the flesh-colored mesh inner lining part. His arm flew up, and he kind of motivated toward the hair system. His wife Duck was by him; she had at that time a hernia bulge in her Rectus sheath. Well, she went to one knee weeping and talking about her hernia she had. Carlier helped her, but he also looked at his hair system blowing down the hill.

SOMETIME ON THEIR WAY OUT of Lotter Cemetery, a mourner would take Bach-Yen the caretaker aside and, looking down at the lawn, go, "Bach-Yen, how do you keep this grass so nice out here? What do you use?"

Old B.Y. would just move her hips and look, as if to say: "Oh, no you don't," and walk off.

Well, Bach-Yen has since gone to the mound herself, so I can tell you it was Kentucky bluegrass she used. No surprises there. Let's face it; if you want quality turfgrass that makes a nice, textured lawn, you go Kentucky bluegrass. What else would she use? St. Augustine's? Not with this hard weather out here! Not even close.

WHEN JOHN DINGER BECAME the center on the Henrytown High basketball team, Coach Lord Futo Tapely got to really simplify his offensive system. Up to then, he'd never had a weapon like that, a legitimate big man like that. For years, he'd tried to run a real complex shuffle offense that featured things like staggered weave-screening, V-cutting, back-cutting, hand-offs, and faking and shifting around of different kinds. His players, bless their hearts, worked hard to learn the shuffle, but they never did. They were nice enough kids. The problem was you didn't have a lot of talent coming out of Henrytown in those days.

But when John Dinger showed up, it was a new story for Lord Futo.

The system Lord Futo implemented was a basic 4-1 set, where they come down, the guards and forwards work the ball around the perimeter for a while—nothing fancy, just good, crisp chest passes, working the ball around—then they dump it down in the low post to Dinger, he turns around, and goes for a dunk shot.

And that was it.

That was the Coach Lord Futo Tapely offensive system. And they did that pretty much every trip down the floor to great effect for four years with Dinger at the center position.

After the team started collecting some wins, the community wondered why the team bothered to work the ball on the perimeter at all. They felt the games were too low scoring because of all the perimeter passing. "Why not just throw it in to the Dinger kid right off?" they said. "The kid could score a hundred if you let him."

"Well, that's not the system, is it?" Lord Futo said, pointing at the court. "Believe me. At least look me in my face, please. That's not the system. The system is we bring the basketball up, the five goes down under the basket and kind of moves around there; the one, two, three, and four work the ball on the perimeter—very important part of the system, you see, working the ball on the perimeter—then eventually they dump it down to the low post, the five catches the ball, turns around, and goes for the dunk shot. *That* is the system, the Lord Futo system. And that's *all* it is."

It was a simple and effective system, but these were high school kids, you remember. So sometimes a

Henrytown guy would launch some sort of a long set shot, you know, or dribble off his foot trying to drive the lane or something. But right away, Lord Futo would bite the problem in the ass, call for time, gather up his boys, and remind them of the system, even if they were way ahead in the ball game. "Stick to the system," he'd say. "This is, in fact, a *real* system, I promise you. When you're out on that floor, don't start acting like we don't have a system. Don't fart around with the basketball. I hope to God you can see what I'm talking about. Look, none of you is a coach. You haven't ever been a coach, and this *is* the Lord Futo system no matter what you *think* you're thinking."

And I guarantee you next trip down the floor, Henrytown worked the ball on the perimeter for a good, solid five minutes (good, clean, crisp chest passes), then they'd dump it down into the low post to Dinger, he'd catch it, turn, and make a gentle dunk shot. By the way, that kind of a possession game on the offensive end can be your best defense, too. But then also as insurance on defense you have Dinger camp out under the cylinder and block 97% of shot attempts.

Yeah, however you want to talk about it, however you want to frame it, Dinger simplified the hell out of the game for Lord Futo, that's for sure. Anytime

Henrytown needed a bucket, they got one. They didn't need back-picking, back-dooring, back-cutting—none of that. That's maybe why Coach Lord Futo Tapely liked to emphasize *system* so much like he did. He knew there was nothing area ball clubs could do about John Dinger. I mean, Bement had nobody; Niantic didn't have a guy over six feet; Minonk thought they had something with a six-two guy; even Danville's biggest guy barely come up to Dinger's elbows. Nobody could stop him. No one could come up with an answer.

The point guard brought the ball up, and he literally passed it to someone who passed to someone else, and so on—meanwhile Dinger set up shop in the low post, and he moved around in the lane with his hand up in the air—and the ball got worked around on the perimeter literally for five minutes—sometimes eight minutes, a whole quarter—but at some point the ball got dumped down in the low post—it didn't have to be a great pass; you could really just literally heave it up in the lane some place, it didn't matter—John Dinger caught the ball, turned, and made the most gentlest dunk shot you ever saw.

YETUNDE HAD THE AQUA NET SPRAY pointed at the side part of her hairdo, and she was moving her arm; she had finger-waves going up the side. Her bangs were combed down against her forehead.

Her finger was pushing the nozzle down, and she moved her arm. She shook the Aqua Net can. She brought it right to her bangs and pushed the nozzle and held it down; her finger was all wet. She moved her arm and sprayed the front, top, and sides generally.

She looked sideways in the mirror; she was holding the Aqua Net can at waist level. Her finger was up off the nozzle and pointed out; you could see it was a red ring where she'd been pushing the nozzle. All her nails were painted up. She held up a mirror in the air so she could see the back part of her hairdo in the big mirror; the long back part was soft and yellow. She put down the mirror and sprayed the sides more.

From: PASTOR MILLER CAINES <pastormillercaines@hotmail.com>
To: Ads <ads@henrytowncrier.com>
Subject: AD PLACEMENT/QUOTE NEEDED

Date: Sat, 28 June 2008 09:54:55

Hello Publisher,
I will like to post a pet ad in your newspaper for 8weeks:

AD TEXT:

Female and male English Bulldog puppies and a male and female yorkie Puppies for Adoption,for more Info.,email pastormillercaines@hotmail.com

I will like you to advise back for the quote of the ad for the period of
8weeks and I will be making payment with my Credit Card

Your Response Will be Highly Appreciated

Address: 7930 Ogden Avenue Lyons IL 60534

phone # 206-339-7093

OUT IN THE CORNFIELD during the early phase of Antietam, the left flank of the 4th Texas Infantry (Wofford's Brigade, Hill's Division, Longstreet's Command) encountered a seven-foot robot. This won't be in your almanacs. Don't *even*.

It happened during a quiet moment, if such a thing could have been found that morning. The left flank of the 4th heard stirs from the leftward rear and, naturally, they assumed it was friendly Confederate forces moving into a shoring up position.

They were just *dead* fucking wrong.

There was a heavy surge of Union fire that was going all over the Rebs' heads and, lo, when they turned and looked, they beheld a giant, hissing, eight-and-a-half-foot metal man waddling forth through the dew-dampened stalks. It was him; it was robot. Union mini-balls were bouncing off him like you bounce peanuts off a fat guy's ass.

From: Ads <ads@henrytowncrier.com>
To: PASTOR MILLER CAINES <pastormillercaines@hotmail.com>
Date: Tue, Jul 1 2008 15:12:22
Subject: RE: AD PLACEMENT /QUOTE NEEDED

Dear Pastor Caines,

We don't publish ads from outside our area. What I'm saying is, your ad won't ever appear in The Crier.

By the way, if somebody in Henrytown wanted a bulldog, they would just walk down to Jim Bearing's and see if he had any for sale. I don't know if he breeds bulldogs or not, but I know he breeds beagle terriers. We place ads for him from time to time. He doesn't have one running right now.

Hey, I see you are a pastor. That's great. Keep it up.

Yours,

Carlier Johnson
Editor and Publisher
(217) 364-3250
carlier@henrytowncrier.com

ALMODAD THE WATERHEAD leaned against the thing. He was wearing black cargo shorts, fur-trimmed opera pumps, and a tiny linen cap with lace frills. Of course the cap was pinned to tufts on the top of his boundlessly gigantic head. Something about the emotions inside the bakery Almodad could just feel made him just feel a very intense feeling of emotions. "I am a vocalist," he said.

"Oh," the cashier said.

"Oh," somebody said.

The song came thundering out of him: one of the old ones. He was immediately committed to giving the most emotional performance of all times. Immediately he was making this huge, huge effort to do really well and give everything inside the bakery.

Some inside the bakery felt he was a troubled vocalist. Some felt he looked sensitive. One wished to ask if there was anything to do. No one thought or was saying it was a public commotion or obvious public raving. They knew inside this was *a display being made.*

The great head purpled.

The baker appeared in the cut.

The baker, live and direct from the cut, thought: What if that darkening head blows apart on the interior of my bakery this morning? That would hurt business. Business *is* being hurt by this as this unfolds, continues to unfold, and unfolds for all times. The bakery business *is* of course being hurt by this . . . . . . But other aspects are perhaps being helped because of this display? Maybe it's of interest to some regulars in the bakery, something obscure like this . . . Gee whiz, the vocalist is going for maximum intensity! The effect is quite interesting of course. Very extreme. I merely wish it had been scheduled ahead of time . . . . Ah, this is a classic "this is a difficult choice for me." Run him out or let it unfold . . . . We're eight minutes in at least of this. We're *a ways* in . . . . . Business *is* being hurt. This may not be reflected in our quarterly performance report. We may not take too bad a hit, but this *is* taking away and *is* now hurting my bakery business. Oh my god! he has just slammed his head down upon the tip jar! The jar is blasted apart. The jar is disintegrated. The jar and its contents is powder. People have scattered. The vocalist is bleeding from the head . . . . He is ruining my business. This is a health violation. Business is being driven down and hurt. This is eating into my savings account. The quarterlies are complete shit . . . . . My health is failing. I have not long to live. I have nowhere to turn for money. I have no money at all anymore and my family is all dead . . . . I'm goddamn ruined. My bakery has been burned to the ground . . . . My family is dead from a disease and interred in the local graveyard. I'm homeless myself and half-dead from diseases without anywhere to turn for money and they will not approve me for insurance . . . . My business has closed its doors and was later burned, and my regulars are loyal to another bakery, the dumb one in Blue Mound . . . . This has gone on long enough for my taste. He stands on the graves of my loved ones and in the ashes of my business. He has ruined the lifeblood of all of this community. This community is finished. We're all finished. He is shitting on my children's gravestones as he stands doing a bunch of these puke noises, gouging his head on the thing. He has managed to destroy everything meaningful. I can't tell what's up or down . . . . All I hear is a voice saying to grab the people left inside the bakery and choke them and crush their windpipes. "Take their lives," I'm told by it. "Then go do home invasions." I have killed people and the ones I love were killed and now I'm dead also. Everything was taken away, including my family and my business. My life partner and my children are in a graveyard. They were fatally injured in a home invasion and buried in a mass grave. I'm alone in a forest of doom. I can't accept another letter from the health inspectors. I have no livelihood. I don't have a job and I have no references . . . . My regulars have set up shop in Blue Mound. I hope they die. I hope these fucks get home invasions. They're hypocrites. They're materialistic. I was always approached and told things that are supposed to make me accept them for coming to my bakery? They are no longer meaningful to me. I will never think they are really true . . . . *I'm finished* . . . I can't get a sense . . . . I don't get any more of course. I don't go anywhere. I don't get to go for visits. I don't see anymore. I don't get to be included. I'm not attending that for there has been no invite.

Overview

The Village of Henrytown is currently creating an inventory of potential sites and buildings which may be available to market to prospects.

Contact:
Almodad Butter-Huggins Reinhart
Economic Development Advisors of Central Illinois
almodreinhart@aol.com
Ph. 217-682-2410

YEARS AND YEARS AGO, I bade Henriette Lightbody make me a duck decoy and crow call. I cut her a check, wrote my driver's license number across on it, and held it out in the air. She took it between her pointer and long fingers. This was in her workshop behind her home this happened.

Henriette was gentle as a bag of minnows and round as a bag of minnows. Was she a large woman? Yes, she was. Gun to my head I'd say four bills. What I mean, I respected her size like I did her craft, for she stacked buffet plates like UNO cards, and Lightbody decoys and calls work the best.

O, where in hell is my green-winged teal hen sleeper, Henriette Lightbody? What about my black walnut crow call? My check was good, yet you cashed it not. You said I'd have my order in a few weeks, but I never had it. I'm sitting here wondering why I never had it. You're now dead and I don't expect anything to change.

FANCY BALDAR STEADY LOOKING at the little snapshot of himself stepping tossing the lawn jart. He looked at the actual lawn jart, at his face, at his body parts, at his cream-colored, semi-formal tunic. He was sitting at the table doing this; he was slumped down. Light was reflecting off the picture.

Light was reflecting off the placemat. His chef salad was caving in and spreading out across there. Fancy was holding the picture in his fingers. He was looking at it every night.

Before bed, he wedged his wheelchair against the back door; he piled all the kitchen chairs. It was a tower of chairs. He drew back; his arm was bent behind him a little. "Wow," he said.

PACO WILLARD HAD HIS TONSILS OUT in 1987. The surgeon's hair was all wet; the hair itself was pushed over to one side of society.

Post-op, they placed the tonsils in a jar to give to Paco to take. He was holding the jar like this on the way home. He got home and wrapped an elastic bandage around, so now—the only way—he had to look up through the bottom if he wished to see the tonsils as they floated all in the alcohol. It was the only way he could.

In 1997, he held it up and looked, and the tonsils were along the bottom of it and coming apart. They were at least softening, it seemed like, he could see.

MARTY-NEIL WILLARD WAS ENJOYING an adult videotape at his home when the front door crashed open and it was a spaceman with glowing red eyes standing there. He fell upon Marty-Neil and started knocking him down.

Marty-Neil noticed the spaceman had a nice odor. Marty-Neil could hear the video playing in the background; somebody on there was griping, "Aww, you said you were gonna bend it. Why didn't you bend it like you said you were gonna?"

The red-eyed man kept launching Marty-Neil against the wall. He performed a leg sweep on Marty-Neil and went upstairs. Marty-Neil heard a bunch of crashing around, and his radio contact equipment came flying down the stairs every so often.

Marty-Neil looked at the TV; somebody was waving his wiener in the air and kinda slumping down; the woman collaborator was standing on a file cabinet kicking her legs at the camera.

The spaceman came down and got in Marty-Neil's pan and told him, "We are going to destroy the mayor.

We have his joint checking account number, and we have his billfold. We are going to bring him to his knees financially."

"Don't!" Marty-Neil said. "They got mouths to feed."

"The children are mostly adults now. They have moved out."

"No, they got like about seven still under that roof. They got, let me see, Madison, Clayton, Hunter, Haley—"

All the sudden Marty-Neil got drowned out by the TV, which went to full volume via some unexplained means.

The camera was panning across a whole group on there now. You had a shot of the wiener-waver from before standing there looking down, hammering away on somebody—now it was a different collaborator, *not* the woman from the file cabinet; she wasn't even in the scene anymore.

AMBER KUSNETSOV WAS THE BRAINY ONE. Except one day she was all the sudden acting aloof in her class. She sat in the back row with a weird look, not raising her hand, and everybody was sort of thinking, "*Huh?*" She got a seventy-two on her biology quiz, which was unheard of. I mean, oh, you talk about little Courtney Kusnetsov or big Gage Kusnetsov ("Twelve Gage" as he's called), and seventy-two's par on the course, but not for Amber. *Not* for Amber. No one could tell what was wrong—not even her boyfriend, whom we shall call Pradip Tenarvitz.

Amber didn't turn up at home for dinner that night. Her brothers and sisters hadn't seen her since school. Pilar called over to the Tenarvitz's. Pradip hadn't seen her. Speedy was awful warm and he got on the other phone and cussed Pradip. Pradip's going, "Huh? I don't—what the? I can't—*huh*?" He was all looking around. His shirt was nice and tucked in—Pradip's. Nobody could find Amber Kusnetsov—not even, like I said, Pradip.

Well, that same night, a couple local fishermen seen Amber, or somebody maybe fitting her description a little bit, assume a Martian form and walk into the woods north of Edda Pond. The Martian had multiple tentacles and a big balloon-like head coming up and surging around in the air. The fisherman saw strange lights flash and heard futuristic, space age buzzing and laser sounds. Then a saucer rose up and shot off in the air.

One of the fishermen got right on the cell phone and got Carlier Johnson down at the *Crier* and told him, hoping he might want to run something about it. Carlier was at his desk; he sat holding the phone on the side part of his face, holding an inkpen in his fingers.

Well, word spread about the fishermen and the alien and the UFO and Amber Kusnetsov's simultaneous disappearance and, over the next days and weeks, others came forward to report sightings of their own, especially Marty-Neil Willard, who claimed to have had coffee with the hot air balloon-head Martian creature; Marty-Neil had been doing some emailing. A lot of emails coming into Village Hall and to the paper. People wanted to know whether it had been a temporary mutation or just abduction with an alien imposter placed in Amber's stead. And *then* what had happened. People around town started to kind of connect the dots in their minds.

TO BIG BOB'S TUMULUS. Nertornartok rode around the tumulus holding his carbon fiber javelin up out in front of himself. His hairdo was pinned back.

He retrieved pewter headband from his totebag. He rode forward and around. He placed headband on his you-know-where.

Pretty soon, he was standing up on his machine doing intervals. In between, he was eating the food.

Headband making the hairpins dig into Nertornartok's frontal scalp area. His arms were sticking straight forward. He was pushing *beyond his own threshold.*

Fast-forward two hours: Nertornartok commutes to the off track wagering facility at Metamora to relax and reference his monitors.

GEORGE BELL MATERIALIZED ON THE WALK in front of the post office out of nowhere. He started pacing up and down screaming swear language so loud it made me flinch from clear on the other walk. He appeared to be in a rage-trance, if you know what that is.

“Ho, George,” I said, coming across, “what’s the matter?”

“Where the fuck am I?” he said.

“Henrytown,” I said.

“How?” he said, turning in circles, looking. “I was at the ball field.”

“Over to the high school?” I said.

“No, Toronto,” he said. “Exhibition Stadium. I was just *there*!” And he flew off the handle. He was bent in half screaming a bunch of stuff about Bruce Kison, the old no-name right-hander from Boston. “He been throwing at us all day! When he bean me, I go at him. Make no mistake. I go at him! I *must* go at Kison.”

While George was carrying on, I saw Mayor Speedy Kusnetsov and Randy Pflum the mortician come out of Village Hall and look over. They were looking right at George. I actually *saw* this. I made a sort of gesture to them like everything was OK. Speedy leaned over to Randy and said something. The former had some documents in his hand and a sweat stain down his golf shirt. I kept making gestures to them and looking at them.

I looked back and saw George was looking at me very intensely. It was upsetting, but I never had the feeling he was mad at me personally. In fact, I was more convinced than ever that what he was going through really had to do with Bruce Kison.

And then Kison materialized out of thin air on the walk next to George. Now, please don't ask how I could recognize Kison; I just could. It was all obvious. And Kison, without hesitation, smacked George across the head with his ball glove, and George's no-flap batting helmet fell on the walk and bounced.

George's hair was all kinda dented. He went with a jumping kick toward Kison's breadbasket, which failed, because Kison sidestepped his man and leveled him with a massive, massive haymaker.

Then, right as the haymaker landed, they vanished. Both of them. George *and* Kison. Gone. I'm standing there looking around. I look up and look at

Speedy and Randy and I gesture to them a couple times. I think I was basically pointing around with my fingers was what I was doing.

I run up the sidewalk at a decent clip to confirm with them guys that they had seen the ball players vanish like I had, because I saw them looking right there.

Randy goes, "I don't know. I couldn't get the angle. My line of sight wasn't the best, so I don't know… I couldn't see…it…I wasn't able……" And he gestured to that effect. Randy wasn't real used to looking at people that weren't on a slab, that weren't dead. He was a mortician.

Speedy said something too, but as he did, a guy on a Harley went by and I didn't hear him. Before I could ask him to repeat himself, he went quickly up the street with his documents.

THERE WAS THIS HALF-TROLL used to live in a kind of teepee by the crick at Minonk. He used to like to sit in a lawn chair right outside and learn hit songs on French horn. He'd set there with cans of warm beer and his cassette player, working out the different melodies.

Well, one day, the half-troll had an email from the lawyer with the news saying the half-troll's mother had passed, and she had left him the apartment complex she ran up in Naperville. So, he was going to have to move up there and manage the complex, is what the lawyer said in the email. It was his mother's wishes.

So, on the half-troll's last day in Minonk, he was sitting by the crick trying to work through a song on the French. It was boxes of his belongings stacked up outside the teepee. He was carrying on and saying things and looking at the horn.

Here comes Old Lookie on his adult tricycle, and he heard the half-troll crying so hard, and Lookie came up. The half-troll told him about the lawyer's e-mail.

"I really see it as a new chapter for you," Lookie said thoughtfully. "Look at it like a good opportunity. Look at it like it's a new chapter. Make your goals a reality."

"Don't act like that," the half-troll told him. "Because they'll email *you* sometime, and then you'll end up my neighbor up in Naperville. You'll come work for me."

Lookie was sitting on his tricycle; he pedaled forward a little bit. "But anyhow, Paul, don't you play that old 'Open Arms' on your French? I'd like to hear that a last time before you go forever."

The half-troll got overcome with emotion and looked around. He chugged a warm beer.

"That's OK," Lookie said. "Go in the teepee and play. I'll stay out here and listen if you don't like to play in front of people. You don't have to play in front of people. Take your beer in there with you. Go ahead. Go in the teepee. I'll stay here."

The half-troll sat in the lawn chair and carried on. "I used to see you on these back roads," he said, crying so hard. "I used to sit in my lawn chair all the days. But now all's I do is live in Naperville."

"Paulie, play me that old 'Open Arms.' Don't do this. Go in your teepee and play it on your French, please."

The half-troll kept looking around. He was overcome with emotions. He pounded a warm beer. "Word has come from Naperville. It has come by email," he said.

Lookie charged forward on his tricycle and plowed into the half-troll and knocked him out of the lawn chair. He was flopping around in the beer cans. The horn was under him; the cassette player was on the side.

Lookie got down off his tricycle and got down in the beer cans with his friend. Lookie was screaming *Go in the teepee* a hundred times. The half-troll was carrying on so bad he was having a fit; he was on top of the horn. Lookie acted like he was having a fit, too, and he was yelling *Go in the teepee.*

SO-AND-SO TURNED into a serpent and went up a gob pile and did yoga, it looked like. It was doing warm-ups.

DURING THE AUTUMN, HERE, LET'S, here's Queen Mother Brard watching her programs, and she was up in her navy chair; looking to us a little dark in there.

What was, here let's, what was Phil Donahue transmitting? Queen Mother had some extra time and she was looking at Phil Donahue and he was *doing* his transmitting. If you have any extra time maybe you could let us know. If you have any extra time you could let me know how Phil Donahue could be so many things at once. I'll meet you for coffee and you can help tell me. Because he is like transmitting and maintaining through the sweeping gesture with informational cards in his hand. The head angled back with that large soft-ass microphone; the middle, ring, and little finger of that other hand sticking out into the studio, over the audience's head. The gesture and remarks seem to us to fuel the program. This is what it's about.

Queen Mother's leg, here, let's, is asleep from being in a tucked under position while she was watching the Phil Donahue program. Phil's body capsule walks never limiting his intuition ascending in his audience clutching his informational cards. This is what it's about for her and for us, too. The cards, and now there's a commercial break. And now there's a commercial.

Queen Mother dragging the leg out. Her male helper is moving in. The helper moves in + Queener places the sleep foot down by the ottoman: The *whole* leg buckles, Lord. The beloved helper keeps moving over there. The whole leg buckles, Lord; whole leg destroyed, Lord. All only blazing leg-misery left for the heaped queen wailing in anguish when the leg woke up again.

The male helper is moving to attend. It was a long way to the navy chair. The servant's little headgear tilting as he moves closer and closer from a long way; he adjusted. He's arriving.

Some people act like horses, Lord, and only think about being *right* by the trough.

A LONG-HAIRED MAN was behind the hardware. The hardware was out of business by now but the Dumpster was still behind it.

The man had made a Dumpster fire and was now and again looking at the fire. "I'm a inventor," he was screaming. "I *been* a inventor! That's what I'm talking about! That's what I'm talking about...*right*...*there*!" and he pointed at the fire using his fingers.

He was holding a ball cap in his hand and kind of jumping around; his hair was flying around.

He took a quick look in the Dumpster at the actual burning garbage itself. He was all wound up and he said, "Oh yeah, that's what *I'm* talking about! I *been* a inventor! I *been* a inventor!"

A COUPLE DAYS BEFORE CHRISTMAS, Yetunde took Marty-Neil to the Star Market to pick out a bird for dinner.

Marty-Neil was out in the snow, right out of range of the automatic doors, acting pretty squirrelly. His J.E.B. Stuart was pressed on the window; there were cold droplets of precipitation *within* beard.

Yetunde and Hwang were talking it out by the checkstand; Hwang said: "Yetty, I can't have him come into the store in his underpants. The Star Market is a family-oriented market. You have surely seen my ad in the paper? The ad says it plainly: family-oriented."

"That's longjohns," she said. "He don't wear underwear." She was right about that—it was longjohns with Marty-Neil. She said, "He wanted to help pick out a bird for his Christmas dinner."

"I'm sorry," Hwang said. "But I can see the shape of his genitalia."

"I want five minutes," Yetunde said. "It would mean the world to him. Can't nobody see."

"I'm so sorry," Hwang said.

At that moment, Marty-Neil made his move. Coming through the automatic doors, beard swelling, he got sideways and squeezed by an old guy pushing a cartload of light bulbs. He cut up through checkstand one past produce on his way to the deli. As he rounded the end cap between aisles three and four a-going full-bore, he bowled over a child—probably a Kusnetsov—like he was Bronko Nagurski coming off-tackle. I think it was all right because the child had kind of a big skull and no permanent damage resulted.

Hwang flew up aisle six to head off Marty-Neil—it's about beating your man to a spot on the floor, as you probably know. Hwang picked his way past some patrons and sideswiped Marty-Neil, bringing him to the linoleum like he was, well, Bronko Nagurski. Big Bronk played both sides of the ball.

You know, about three, four times a year, I sit in my kitchen with some food and think: If the real Bronko had tackled himself, would it have caused a vortex? I don't know. I can't figure it out in my mind right now. Of course, Bronko Nagurski is long dead, so if this gets figured out, it's going to be *in a mind.* It's not something you could test.

Well, I go too fast. Perhaps, you *could* go out to

Saint James Cemetery at International Falls and get up Bronko's remains and try to induce a vortex. What you do is, go to a laboratory, scoot the remains into two piles, get up some in each hand, clap together hard as you can, and then wait on a vortex. Doing that, you may get it figured out. But beware: You're going to be in lawsuit territory. I hope you realize that. That is, you'd have a hell of a time with the Nagurski family on it, but you just tell them: "Science is damn hard business. This is science, Nagurski's Loved One. Now, look, I can leave the remains in my garage or I can FedEx you the remains and bill you for the cost or you can wire me the money. I suppose I can take a personal check but please understand I'll have to hang onto the remains until the check clears, because I can tell you one thing, and I'm quite serious on this point: I am not about to take a bath on shipping and handling. Not even close. Not even *close* to that. That being said, what it comes down to is, I want to do the right thing. I hope you can understand that. I know you suffered a loss and an inconvenience and that's OK, except you need to meet me halfway on this. We've all made some mistakes in this life. Let's just get this figured out the right way and move on."

You could say that to them. You could really do

this. You could become this kind of scientist.

Hwang worked at pinning his man down. True, portions of the wet beard did fall into Hwang's mouth. And the padlock Marty-Neil kept on his longjohns gouged Hwang's nards disagreeably.

During the struggle, Hwang's loafer flew off and knocked down some cans of soup, which fell down and sort of rolled.

2.0 Incident Description

2.1 Pre-Incident Activities

Operations at the plant were normal in the hours before the incident. At approximately 10:30 p.m., just moments before the incident, all PVC1 reactors were making PVC except for reactor D306, which was being cleaned.

2.2 Incident

A few minutes after 10:30 p.m, workers throughout the plant heard a very loud rumbling and some smelled VCM. The shift supervisor and operators in the south (Paste) end of the reactor building heard the Paste section deluge alarm, indicating deluge system activation in that area.

The shift supervisor left the Paste control room to check the VCM gas detection system reading. The shift supervisor stated that two areas had levels above the instrument's measurable limit, suggesting a large release. He said that on his way to investigate the release, he walked past an open doorway in the PVC1 area near the reactor D310 and saw material spraying from the bottom of D310 and a foaming mixture on the floor about 1.5 feet deep. He immediately climbed the stairs to the upper level.

According to the shift supervisor, operators on the upper level of PVC1 reported that the pressure on the reactor D310 was rapidly falling. He informed two operators that he had seen material spraying from the bottom of D310 and they immediately began checking the valves and controls for D310. The supervisor and one operator tried to go to the lower level through an interior stairwell, but high VCM concentrations forced them to retreat.

The shift supervisor instructed operators to open vent valves on reactor D310 to relieve pressure and slow the release. At this point, he saw that the reactor pressure had already dropped to 10 psi, further indicating a large release.

Attempting again to go to the lower level, the shift supervisor descended an exterior stairway when a series of explosions occurred. The explosion knocked over two 3,000 gallon VCM recovery tanks; lifted multi-ton dryers off their supports; and destroyed the laboratory, safety, and engineering offices (Figure 1).

The ensuing fire spread to the PVC warehouse west of the reactor building, burned for hours, and sent a plume of acrid smoke into the community (Figure 4).

Four operators were killed by the explosions: two working near the top of the reactor and two working on the lower level. A fifth operator died in the hospital two weeks later. The shift supervisor and two workers were hospitalized, and four workers were treated at the scene.

2.3 Incident Aftermath

2.3.1 Community Impact

The fire sent a plume of acrid smoke into the community (Figure 4). In response, emergency responders evacuated approximately 150 residents living within one mile of the plant and the Illinois State Police closed the major roadways in the area.

EMBARGOED UNTIL TUES., 3/6/07 9:00 a.m.. CT/10:00 a.m. ET

A FEW MINUTES AGO, I KEPT envisioning Bad Willie's partus; I kept having of it this natural, repeated envisioning. I'm saying, me as an adult being up in the birth room seeing it for my own eyes; looking at him on the warming table, with his crippled arms and all his everything else.

Someone asks, "Why not envision Hwang's partus repeatedly? Is there something so terribly uninteresting about Hwang's partus?"

I say, "Think of Hwang as infant; there's a *ton* to like there."

Someone asks, "What about Hwang on the warming table?"

I say, "Yeah, go to *his* partus. Go to *that* room, *that* area. Whatever I'm going through, go *there.* I must lay it down in Hwang's birth room, Hwang's partus area. I must put in the hours. If there is another way, tell me. But think now, you, of adult Hwang at home doing his *Bodies in Motion* exercise videotapes."

Someone asks, "Is he 'walking it out?'"

I say, "He is 'lifting the knee'; he is 'driving the knee up.'"

Someone asks, "Is he 'pushing it up?'"

I say, "He is 'pushing it out.'"

Someone asks, "Is he 'inhaling up?'"

I say, "Uh-huh, and he is 'exhaling down.'"

Someone asks, "Is he 'kicking it out?'"

I say, "He is 'taking it out.'"

Someone asks, "Is he 'jumping rope?'"

I say, "He is 'walking it out.'"

Someone asks, "What if I wish Bad Willie was in the room?"

I say, "If it makes you feel good to put Bad Willie in the room, put him in the room."

You can see Hwang steady preempting *Bodies in Motion*. He is certainly preempting the background exercisers, and sometimes he is even preempting Gilad. Sometimes, the background exercisers don't look like they know what's coming, like there was no rehearsal. You can see them look over. There is hesitation on their part. You can see them looking at Gilad when he changes the movement. You can see how they're hesitating.

GLORIA-HALF-OF-SOMETHING knocked down a gelding and cored out his rectum like a foot and a half.

When she finished, she took off across down the hard road toward Bement—although I don't believe Gloria *was on her way* to Bement. It could be I don't even need to point this out anymore. It could be it was obvious already. We are all getting to know each other so well by now. We don't think she was going to Metamora, either, do we?

Turn your head now, and look at it caper across in the air: the mighty wampus cat's fabled, twinkling, Christmas tree light, lily-white bunghole! The fugitive bunghole!

PACO'S BIOLOGICAL WENT ON DIALYSIS. This was in Texas; he hadn't been in Henrytown for thirty years.

And he would be having his dialysis at the center. And he'd be sitting watching *Little House*. Half-pint and Mary would be up there; Pa would be up there; Doc Baker would be; Mr. Edwards would.

The dialysis machine would be making noise, have different lights, the screen. Paco's biological's arm would be on the table. It was blood in tubes going through the machine and Paco's biological would be sitting there, looking up. Some of the blood would be in tubes; some of it would be in him. Some would be getting ready to leave in the tubes, and some of it would be coming back in his arm.

If you wanted, you could have gotten up and looked out the window and seen the shopping center across the street; you could have seen Texans in the parking lot over there.

Here,

tubes, him,
do.
Arm,
tubes.
There,
little tubes, Reverend Alden.

Paco's biological had a Texas woman: Paco's-biological's-war-department. She was the one drove him to the dialysis center. She had one of these real low, long butts you see out here. And she was a wonderful person.

She'd be there, looking. She'd be in the room, looking at him; she'd be looking like she'd be. The machine would be standing there, making noise. And people in other areas of Texas would be doing fine, leading their normal lives.

His woman would be reaching up with her fingers, "Let's see what's on now." After while, she'd get her jacket and walk across to the shopping center. You could have gotten up and looked out the window and watched Paco's-biological's-war-department go into the shopping center, the whole way.

By near end of his dialysis, she would be back in the room with him. You could hear people in the other room getting set up for their dialysis or having their dialysis. You could hear the technicians.

Paco's biological would be having bladder tightness. He would be starving. He would want the TV off. He would be exhausted sitting there, looking up, head hanging down forwards.

LITTLE BRACKEN DOWN THE DRIVEWAY toward Grampa Boles. Grampa Boles in the street. Pile of leaves burning there. You could hear the wheels on Little Bracken's aluminum walker on the pavement. "I'm not—Grampa, I'm unsure what I'm supposed to be doing right now."

Grampa Boles in the street looking at Little Bracken coming; Little Bracken toward him, and toward the leaves. You could smell the leaves.

The light-duty rake Grampa Boles held was touching the pavement. He looked over. He said something; his head moved. You could see the leaves. He kept raking the side of the pile; you could hear the sound of that. The rake was dragging across on the pavement. You could see Little Bracken.

OLD LOOKY'S GHOST ONCE TOLD ME: "Look, look, an artichoke farm! Look at those sand dunes in the background. It's overcast. It's kind of chilly. I'll sit over here and feel it in the field of my own eardrums and enjoy it."

I said, "Well."

He said, "Know in your heart it's not some impossible thing to ask. It's an artichoke farm, not the end of the world. Now, please, hand me that food."

HWANG ON HIS WAY from his workout at Danville Racquet Club one morning, when he come upon a crowd of forty aliens on the interstate standing there, chatting, and gesturing. They were taking up the whole road.

Hwang pulled up, and eleven of the aliens waved to him. Hwang looked around; he was pretty emotional. The aliens were kind of stumpy and had these big, see-through heads; the sun was coming through their heads. Their heads looked so delicate to him; he didn't want to drive in there and burst all their heads open.

"Hi," said one of the spacemen, suddenly right by Hwang's ear—four aliens had come over to the driver's side window. Hwang looked without moving his head. The one leaned in on him; his gigantic blue head was inside the window; the organs in his head was tilting to one side. "I like hoping we're not delaying you so much after your workout," said the one; then his head vibrated a little bit.

Hwang saw through the head the other thirty-six

aliens chatting and carefully going along to the shoulder of the interstate.

The vibrating head was touching the steering wheel. "Touch my head," said the alien, his voice faltering, "and I'll give you thirty dollars."

LET HER THROUGH, PLEASE. Step back, please, Sir. Thank you, please. She's coming out of the dining area.

She's on top of the carpet in front of us. She's standing on top of carpet in front of one of the gentlemen of our new community. She's over by that gentleman who is wearing what are apparently pleated corduroy trousers.

Let's all quietly notice things for a while: her face and head, for instance. And I *do* agree with you, Miss; her hair *is* straighter. You could tell from the pictures, perhaps.

Yes, you can ask her something, but one at a time. Listen to her respond before you ask another question. Give her time to respond. If she gets overwhelmed like that she'll get on the roof of the complex.

Now she's sitting down. Is that right? Is she sitting? What is she doing? Sir, step back. She wants to watch TV.

From: "Shannon Crowe" <shi@metatech.com.sg>
To: Ads <ads@henrytowncrier.com>
Date: Sun, 5 Apr 2009 23:59:05
Subject: I offer you friendship.

Hi my new friend!

My name is Ekaterina I hope my letter will find you in good mood. II for the first time try such way of dialogue, and I really do not know what to tell right now even that I understand that this first message is of great importance. But I have decided to write to you and maybe you will answer. I sincerely hope that you are looking for the same. Once upon a time, the loneliness has come into my home and since then does not want to let me off. I freeze from loneliness.

Every evening I look at a sundown and I try to absorb all warmth of day, up to last drop. I am looking for a partner in life to share simple pleasures and together take off from the soul the weariness and sadness given. I am looking for a man to become friends first of all and to go together along the road of life, to have common joy, together enjoy autumn magnificence, together the future. I do not know if it is really possible to find it in such a way. But I know that many people not been able to find happiness in the usual life, have found happiness in this way. I am happy where I now, and my life is a good life, but happiness has no sense if you cannot share it with person dear to you. I could not find here a man who will make me blossom like flower. That is why I took this courageous for me step.

As speak, the journey of a thousand miles begins with a single step. Neither of us knows to where this path will lead but I am willing to walk it and see where it takes us.

I tried to put my picture in my profile, but I understand nothing in computers and I did something wrong. But I will send my picture through e-mail if you will answer.

Please reply only to my personal e-mail:
ekaterina2129@gmail.com

Bye.

IT COME TO MY MIND, IF IT ENDS UP you don't make it, or you missed a part, I could call you on the cell phone and we could have a little talk about all this. I could let you know and charm you, on the phone. I think it would have to be a series of calls, but I could still do it. It'd be best to have, like, four calls for the whole thing. Not my first choice, but. I'd rather do it this way, but. Mother used to say there's another kind of side to me; she'd say that then *come after me*! I could still do it, and it really don't matter where it is. I'm on some little bit different.

And Mother used to say, "I don't want to physically *organize* big, continuous banquets of special words to get somebody to pay attention! Do we need to have a big-old, flashing website? But *you...*" This was often said. Well, I kind of added the website part as part of a new visualization of how it used to be. Mother died before websites. Mother died at Lincoln Manor facility in Danville probably ten years before real websites.

That facility is closed now, and gone. I don't *know* what. It actually closed five years after Mother died, seems like right around when they transmitted that they had found Amber Kusnetsov. Who could forget the afternoon that *that* was transmitted, and the emotion you had in your minds when that had happened to you? But when Lincoln Manor *did* close, you want to know what happened? I guess the owner of the facility decided to stop paying the bills. They got a call one day at the front desk. At the time of it, no one knew why, but the residents all the sudden had forty-eight hours. The next couple days, vans and representatives from facilities all over the region showed up to help transition and relocate the residents. Lincoln Manor staff members was being calm as possible, but I don't know if it was working. The residents didn't know where they were going, and they were looking around bumping along in their wheelchair. They had forty-eight hours. And the employees had forty-eight; everybody had forty-eight. They *were given* forty-eight.

Mountains upon mountains of clouds out the window in the middle of the entire summer, and then the TV. Mother would point out something, that was, "My life straight-up ain't *no* one's personal restroom," then, half the time, she'd *come after me*! Well, she *would* have, anyway.

Dear Crier Staff:
Sorry I was on vacation.
I am trying to leave Henrytown so I will only renew the newspaper for 3 months.
Sorry for not continuing the newspaper but I want to leave Henrytown.
Montez

JOHN DINGER WENT TEN MINUTES outside Henrytown over to Niantic to kill trolls. He went in to see the village board president, who said, "Obviously, we're experiencing this troll problem," and he had his fingers like this and was gesturing. "The reason it's a problem is they are killing our citizens, the citizens of Niantic."

When the meeting had started, Dinger fit in the office—he was all hunched down, but he had fit; he was nodding. But by ten minutes in, he had gotten too big; he had to go outside and talk to the board through the window. It's OK; it didn't have to be a real formal meeting because the details had been worked out on email.

Dinger went out, reconnoitered Niantic. He physically walked Niantic and looked at Niantic. He went up on their gob pile and looked at Niantic from there. He stopped in had lunch at the new Hardee's. He walked up to the drive-thru and made his formal boast to the employees. The shift leader was so moved he gave Dinger half off his meal. Dinger stood out in the parking lot eating roast beefs two at a time. In the field by the restaurant, he could see a dead Niantic citizen on the ground.

In the afternoon, the trolls ambushed Dinger in historic downtown Niantic. The trolls were good-sized and had him three-to-one but still got their ass routed and killed. Dinger took off his shirt and went to work breaking bones and tearing down eyeballs and crushing troll-dreams. The female one had a tusk coming out—Dinger took and tore that out; he cut the other two in half with it, broke it in pieces, and put most of it down their throats after they were dead. It was a terrible mess out there. He left the corpses on the street and walked home to wash up for his date with Gloria-half-of-something.

When he got home he was the size of his home—no way he could fit into it now, let alone in the tub. He stood in his front yard and looked at the home. He could see in the gutters. He got on the cell phone, called Paco come feed the parakeets.

Dinger walked out to Edda Pond to wash that troll gore off his person, which he did. He stood in the middle of the pond and parted his hair; he looked so nice, just like he was Merlin Olsen. He noticed it was some troll gore stuck in his umbilicus; he scraped it out with his thumb. He got out and went naked into the woods.

When Gloria-half-of-something saw him coming through the trees, she climbed up on a boulder. He came up and started talking about how he had killed the trolls. He brought his wiener close to her. He was rubbing her buttocks and steering his wiener into her. He was bringing it close, *closer*. He was looking down at his wiener, and he was talking about the trolls. He was bringing it closer every second—

Slow, slow,
close,
bring.
Close,
bring wiener,
holding wiener.
Bringing wiener close.

At the same time as this, Hwang and Bad Willie at Hwang's on the davenport. Hwang was softly scratching Bad Willie's back and buttocks area. Bad Willie was lying on his stomach; his bare wiener was pushed against the upholstery of the davenport.

Gloria reached back and clawed Dinger's buttocks and pulled him forward like she wanted him *in* by now. He pushed back and took a step back. He was going to bring that wiener at his own speed.

Hwang lay down, and Bad Willie started rubbing his wiener on Hwang, *up against Hwang*; Hwang kissed him and looked at him.

Dinger started bringing his wiener in. Bringing it in through the air.

Close,
slow, forwards,
looking at it.
Trolls, yes trolls,
forwards.
Close, forwards.

At the same time as this, Henriette and Marty-Neil at Marty-Neil's on the davenport. She had her legs down his beard; she was propping herself for him. Sometimes, he was grabbing the back part of the davenport; sometimes, he had a hold of his own boobs or wiener.

It was when Dinger was bringing it in forwards slow the second time he noticed something twinkle lily white down in front of his wiener—in front of him and a little above where he was originally going with his wiener, namely, Gloria's clitoris.

Marty-Neil squashed his mouth on Henriette's clitoris area.

What was twinkling lily white—what Dinger was looking at—was, of course, Gloria-half-of-something's fabled *actual*; it was her *actual*, honest-to-God, *real life* bunghole, her *literal* bunghole.

Gloria-half-of-something herself didn't know what was going on. She was on the boulder, looking around. Another minute, she was going to turn and rip Dinger's junk.

Marty-Neil shut his mouth and pounded it on Henriette's clitoris.

John Dinger the Large, the giant of Henrytown, got up and took hold of his vast wiener. His head, his hair, was way up in the air, in the trees. He brought his wiener up and placed it on the light; he did not *push it in* the light, as that would be to *put out* the light; no, he *placed it on the light* and rested it there. And he rested it there.

THERE WAS AN AMOUNT OF GULAB TAPELY; I found that amount to be too little.

Now, what's too little?

Five minutes? An hour? Gulab's male gonads in a bag somewhere? A few of her molecules in a dish somewhere?

When she was a boy, she took a lesson on pipe organ. Her tutor stood there, saying, "This one, Gulab, this one. Look at me, please. This one. You see what I'm doing? It's *this* one. No, no, this one, Gulab. What are you doing? I don't understand what you're looking at. Look *here*. Look at *this* one. *This* one, Gulab. *This* one. *This! This! This one!*"

Gulab was sitting in front of the pipe organ in a beautiful little green suit; his head was vibrating. The tutor grabbed Gulab's wrist and pressed his hand onto the keyboard. "*This* one, Gulab. *This* hand."

Gulab got up, ran into the backyard, and lobbed hedge apples onto the neighbor's back deck until the tutor had gone home. Then Gulab came back in and played J.S. Bach on pipe organ for five and a half hours.

A dish of her molecules on the bench and her male gonads on the keyboard itself? Do you need more of Gulab Tapely? Is that what the issue is?

IT WAS SOME MALE JAPANESE INVESTORS (three or so) come to Henrytown. It was thought they could buy up and rebuild what was left of Polk Plastics. That was what the thought was. *It* was thought that. It was thought *they*.

They went out and had a look at the site. They had on hardhats and all the time kept communicating with each other.

Graciela Bearing was out there. Almodad couldn't be there cause he'd injured his head. Graciela had a hardhat on and a nice business suit and was standing waiting for the Japanese investors to finish communicating together. To her mind, it seemed like the investors weren't real impressed with the site. "This tour," she thought, "isn't lasting long enough."

Later on, she treated them to lunch in town. The Japanese investors communicated with each other throughout the meal. Graciela sort of zoned out, and chewed her meal, and looked at the Japanese investors.

"Excuse me," she said at one point. "What do you

think of coming to Henrytown?" She didn't ask about the site itself. To ask about the site was to ask how you did on the tour part; to ask about Henrytown was to leave yourself out of it.

The Japanese investors turned their heads and started to look at Graciela; she completely zoned out and looked at her meal. Her hairdo was sitting there shaped like the inside part of the hardhat.

ABOUT THE AUTHOR

Chris Erickson is from Decatur, Illinois. His writing has appeared or is forthcoming in *The American Reader, Gigantic, Action Spectacle, Capilano Review, Seneca Review, PANK,* benmarcus.com, *The Hobo-Tramp Voice*, and *Byline*. He is the former host of "Boxcar Whitey's Old-Time Music & Lore Progr'm," which aired on KRCL FM Salt Lake City from 2003–05 and on KDRT FM Davis from 2006–08. He is a graduate of the UC Davis Creative Writing Program, and still lives in Davis, CA.

$20.00
ISBN 978-1-938603-33-4